BABY-SITTERS
Little Sister

Karen's Runaway Turkey

Ann M. Martin

THANKS!
This book was
donated by:
CHELSEA BENGE
for her 8th birthday,
10/3/99

ISBN 0-590-52392-9

12 11 10 9 8 7 6 5 4 3 2 1   9/9 0 1 2 3 4/0

Printed in the U.S.A.   40
First Scholastic printing, November 1999

Karen's Wish

"Andrew, pumpkins are orange, not green," I told my little brother in my most grown-up voice.

"I like green," answered Andrew. He continued making a chain of paper pumpkins with green construction paper.

I sighed. "Andrew, no one is going to know those are pumpkins."

"I will know," said Andrew.

Honestly, Andrew can be so stubborn sometimes. He is four going on five. I am seven. My name is Karen Brewer.

Andrew and I were at the kitchen table making Thanksgiving decorations. Even though it was still early November, we were starting to get ready. We wanted to make enough decorations for all the windows in the little house. Maybe even the big house too. (I will explain why Andrew and I have two houses in a minute.) We had crayons, markers, construction paper, glue, tape, and scissors spread out in front of us. I was drawing a picture of a turkey to hang in the kitchen window. Our nanny, Merry Perkins, was stirring a big pot of chili on the stove. It smelled wonderful.

I was having fun, but something was on my mind. I decided to speak up about it. (I am very good at speaking up.)

"You know what, Merry?" I said as I colored in my turkey's feathers.

"What?" answered Merry, turning away from the stove.

"Thanksgiving is unfair to kids," I announced, waving my crayon in the air.

Merry raised her eyebrows. "How is it unfair?"

"Kids are not allowed to do anything important for Thanksgiving." Andrew held up his green pumpkin chain, but I ignored it. "We make decorations and set the table. But we do not do any cooking. I wish I could cook something for Thanksgiving."

"You eat," Andrew reminded me.

"I know I eat," I said. "But that is not the same as cooking."

"Well, you know you are not allowed to use the stove," Merry reminded me. I nodded. "But not all cooking involves the stove," Merry continued.

"Most Thanksgiving cooking does," I said, thinking of turkey and stuffing, sweet potatoes, creamed onions, carrots, beets, pies, and homemade biscuits. In fact, I could not think of any part of our Thanksgiving dinner that was not cooked.

"What would you like to make for your Thanksgiving dinner?" Merry asked me.

"A pumpkin pie," I answered right away. Dessert is my favorite part of most meals.

4

"Well, maybe this year you can make one," said Merry, smiling.

I looked at Merry with wide eyes. "Really?"

"I could teach you how," Merry continued. "You can learn to make the filling and crust. Then all a grown-up has to do is put the pie in the oven for you."

That sounded fine to me. More than fine. And besides, I knew Merry would be a wonderful teacher. She has already taught me lots of things, like how to make a pencil holder out of clay. (Merry teaches a pottery class at the craft center where Mommy works.)

"Can you teach me too?" Andrew asked.

"Sure," said Merry.

"Can we start right away?" I was already putting my crayons back in their box.

"Well, not right now," answered Merry. "I will need to buy the ingredients first. But we can begin tomorrow, when you come home from school."

I could not wait.

Two Kitchens

I tried to concentrate on drawing my turkey. But I could not. I kept thinking about pumpkin pie and how much fun it would be to make one.

The kitchen in my little house is cozy. It has blue-and-white checked curtains, a white stove with a red teakettle on it, a small white refrigerator, a big windowsill filled with Mommy's plants, and a round wooden table where we often eat. It is a good kitchen to cook in because everything is close together. Not like in the big house.

Remember my two houses? Now I will tell you more about them.

First of all, I did not always live in two houses. When I was very little, Andrew and I lived in our big house with Mommy and Daddy, here in Stoneybrook, Connecticut. Then Mommy and Daddy began fighting. At first a little, then a lot. Finally they got divorced. (That means they are not married to each other anymore.) Mommy, Andrew, and I moved out of the big house and into the little house. Daddy stayed in the big house. After all, it is the house he grew up in.

Then Mommy married Seth Engle. That made him my stepfather. I like Seth a lot. When he came to live with us at the little house, he brought his dog, Midgie, and his cat, Rocky.

Daddy married again too. He married Elizabeth Thomas, and she became my stepmother. Elizabeth and her four children came to live with Daddy in the big house. Her children are Sam and Charlie, who go to high school; Kristy, who is thirteen

(Kristy and I are special friends); and David Michael, who is seven like me. They are my stepbrothers and stepsister.

Then Daddy and Elizabeth adopted Emily Michelle from a faraway country called Vietnam. Emily is two and a half and very cute. I named my pet rat after her.

There were so many people at the big house that Nannie, Elizabeth's mother, came to help take care of everyone. Nannie has a candy-making business. She lets me help her make candy. Nannie also helps out with all the pets. There is a puppy named Shannon, a kitten named Pumpkin, and two goldfish. Plus Andrew's pet hermit crab, Bob, and my rat, Emily Junior, are there whenever Andrew and I are.

Andrew and I spend every other month with Mommy in the little house. The rest of the time we live with Daddy.

I made up special names for my brother and me. I call us Andrew Two-Two and Karen Two-Two. (I thought up those names after my teacher read a book to our class. It was called *Jacob Two-Two Meets the Hooded Fang*.) Andrew and I are two-twos because we have two of so many things. We have two houses and two families, two mommies, two daddies, two cats, and two dogs. Plus I have two bicycles, one at each house. And I have two stuffed cats who look exactly alike. Goosie lives at the little house. Moosie stays at the big house. I have two pairs of glasses too. The blue ones are for reading. The pink ones are for the rest of the time. Also, Andrew and I have two sets of clothes, books, and toys. This way, we do not need to pack much when we go back and forth between our houses.

I even have a best friend near each house. Nancy Dawes lives next door to the little house. Hannie Papadakis lives across the street and one house down from the big house. Nancy, Hannie, and I call ourselves the Three Musketeers because we do everything together. We are in Ms. Colman's second-grade class at Stoneybrook Academy.

I could not wait to tell Nancy and Hannie my exciting news. I was sure that when they heard I would be making a pumpkin pie, they would want to cook one too. And you know what? When I learn, I can teach them.

Baked in a Pie

When I came home from school the next day, my little-house kitchen looked different. On the counter were mixing bowls, measuring spoons, jars of spices, milk, sugar, eggs, and some cans with pictures of pumpkins on them.

"I thought you needed a real pumpkin to make pumpkin pie," I said.

"You can use a real pumpkin. But it takes much longer," Merry answered.

"I guess it is easier to use canned pumpkin," I said.

"We were waiting for you before we started," Andrew told me. (Andrew goes to preschool in the morning. He comes home earlier than I do.) "We got out all the things we needed."

"I see," I said. "Thanks." I know how hard it is for Andrew to wait when he is excited about something.

"Do you want a snack before we start?" Merry asked me.

"Uh, no," I said when I saw Andrew's face.

Andrew hopped up and down.

I shrugged off my backpack, hung up my jacket, and washed my hands at the kitchen sink. Finally, I was ready to begin too.

"There are two parts to a pumpkin pie," Merry explained. "The filling and the crust."

"The crust is hard to make, right?" I interrupted. (I have heard Mommy say how difficult it is to cook a really good crust.)

Merry nodded. "Yes, the crust is hard. So today we will begin with the easier part, the filling."

12

I had no idea so many things went into the filling. I was beginning to think our dessert should be called a pumpkin-and-a-lot-of-spices pie. Andrew and I spent a long time measuring out sugar, salt, ginger, cinnamon, and cloves — with Merry's help. Actually, I was pretty good at measuring things. But Andrew needed some help. He kept mixing up the teaspoon with the table-spoon. And he spilled a lot of sugar on the floor. Merry did not mind, though. We were having too much fun.

Andrew mixed all the spices together with a big wooden spoon while I measured out the milk and poured it into the spices. Then we added two eggs and the pumpkin from the cans. Merry had to help us open the cans. But I broke the egg all by my-self without getting any of the shell in the bowl.

When our filling was ready, Merry poured it into a crust she had bought at the grocery store.

"I hope this crust tastes as good as the

homemade kind," I said as Merry put the pie in the oven.

"It should taste almost as good," Merry said, her eyes twinkling. "Remember, this is your first pie."

"When will it be ready?" Andrew wanted to know.

"In about fifty minutes," answered Merry.

"Fifty minutes. That is almost an hour." It is hard for me to wait too. Almost as hard as it is for Andrew.

"It will be ready by the time Seth and your mom come home," Merry said.

And guess what? She was right. Right about Mommy, anyway. Merry was pulling the pie out of the oven when Mommy walked into the house.

"What smells so good?" Mommy wanted to know.

"Our pie!" I cried. Andrew and I ran to Mommy to give her hugs.

"We made a pumpkin pie," Andrew announced.

"Merry is teaching us how to bake," I added.

I had to admit, our pie did look good. The filling had set and turned a deep orange. And it smelled of cloves and cinnamon. I wanted to have a piece right away. But I knew Mommy and Merry would not let me. Mommy is always saying I should not ruin my appetite.

"This year, Andrew and I are going to make the pie for our Thanksgiving dinner," I informed Mommy. Andrew nodded. "And you know, the pie is one of the most important parts of the meal," I added.

Mommy and Merry laughed. But they agreed. After all, what would Thanksgiving be without pumpkin pie?

A Contest

"You made a whole pie yesterday?" Nancy sounded surprised.

"Well, just the filling," I admitted. "The crust was ready-made."

"Did you bring in a piece for us to taste?" asked Hannie.

"We finished it for dessert last night," I said.

"A whole pie?" Hannie could not believe it.

"Everyone had two pieces," I explained.

"Even Andrew. Besides, we gave some to Merry to take home."

"Next time, we want a piece of your pie," said Nancy.

"Even if it gets squished on the way to school?" I asked.

Nancy and Hannie giggled. We were sitting in the back of our classroom waiting for Ms. Colman, our gigundoly wonderful teacher. I looked around the room. Ricky Torres, my pretend husband, and Natalie Springer were already sitting in the front row. During school, I sit in the front row too, because I wear glasses like they do. But before Ms. Colman arrives, I sit in the back with Hannie and Nancy so we can talk.

Addie Sidney zoomed by in her wheelchair. She stopped outside Hootie's cage to feed him. (Hootie is our class guinea pig.)

Bobby Gianelli chased Hank Reubens and Omar Harris around the room. I rolled my eyes. "Bobby is going to get it when Ms. Colman comes in," I said to Hannie and Nancy. I was eyeing the door to Mr. Berger's

18

room. Our classrooms are connected, and when Ms. Colman isn't here, Mr. Berger keeps an eye on our class.

"Omar and Hank are going to get in trouble too," Nancy remarked as Hank knocked over a chair trying to get away from Bobby. (Bobby Gianelli used to be the class bully, but he is not so bad now. At least not most of the time.)

I saw the twins, Tammy and Terri Barkan. Tammy stood near the front of the room talking to Sara Ford. Terri was at her desk playing ticktacktoe with Audrey Green. Pamela Harding sat with her friends Leslie Morris and Jannie Gilbert. The three of them were whispering. Pamela is my best enemy. All she ever does is sit with her friends and gossip. I did not see Ian Johnson. I guessed he must be absent.

"Good morning, class," said Ms. Colman when she arrived.

"Good morning, Ms. Colman," we said. We rushed to our seats.

Ms. Colman asked Pamela to take attendance. Boo and bullfrogs. Taking attendance is one of my favorite jobs. And I already knew that everyone but Ian was here today. Oh, well.

"I have an important announcement to make," said Ms. Colman when Pamela was finished.

I sat up a little straighter in my chair. I love Ms. Colman's announcements. They are always interesting.

"I just received a notice from the Stoneybrook Historical Society. They are sponsoring an essay contest for the first-, second-, and third-graders of Stoneybrook," Ms. Colman began.

Goody, I thought. I love to write.

"Do we get a prize if we win?" Bobby Gianelli called out.

"Yes, but please wait until I am finished making my announcement, Bobby. Then I will tell you about the prizes. And remember to raise your hand."

"Sorry," said Bobby.

"Students who enter the contest must write about a person they are thankful for, then explain how they will show their thanks to that person this Thanksgiving."

"I am thankful for my dog," Ricky said.

"The student with the best essay wins a grand prize," Ms. Colman continued. "I do not know what the grand prize is, though."

Pamela raised her hand. "Are there any other prizes?" she asked when Ms. Colman called on her.

"Yes. Twenty dollars for first prize, fifteen dollars for second prize, and ten dollars for third prize."

"Are we all going to enter this contest?" I asked.

"Yes, I was hoping we would. I would like all of you to write two paragraphs by Friday answering both parts of the question."

Friday was two days away. That gave me plenty of time to write a brilliant essay.

"You will each read your essay aloud to

the class," Ms. Colman continued. "Then I will collect all the essays and send them to the historical society."

"I wonder what the grand prize is," Ricky whispered to me.

I shrugged. I did not really care. It is always fun to win something.

In the Kitchen

I thought writing my essay would be easy. But it was not. For one thing, I could not decide who to write about. There are too many people I am thankful for: Mommy, Daddy, Kristy, Andrew, Seth, Elizabeth, Nannie, Hannie, Nancy. I could go on and on. I was sitting at my desk, but I was not writing. I was twirling my hair and chewing on my pencil. I knew Ricky was writing about his aunt Mabel, who gave him his dog. Hannie had said she would write about her mother. I sighed. I was sure most of the kids in my

23

class would be writing about someone in their family. But most of them did not have two families.

I was glad when Merry came upstairs to ask me if I wanted another pie-baking lesson.

"Sure," I answered. I was ready to stop thinking about my essay for awhile.

"Today we are going to make a piecrust," said Merry when we were all in the kitchen.

I helped Merry get out the flour, salt, and butter. Then I helped Andrew find the other things we needed: a mixing bowl, measuring spoons, a fork, and a rolling pin. "Are you sure this is all we need?" Andrew asked Merry.

Merry nodded. "You need patience to make a good crust. Not too much else."

Before we began, Merry told us not to handle the pastry dough any more than necessary, or it would be tough.

Andrew and I measured out the flour and salt and mixed them together. Then we put in the butter and a little cold water. I mixed everything together with a fork. When I was done, the mixture looked like very tiny peas. Merry said it should look like that.

We were about to roll out the dough when Merry looked at the clock. "Ooh," she said, "it is later than I thought. We will not have time to finish today."

"You mean we cannot roll out the crust?" I said. I was very disappointed.

"Not today," Merry replied. "And tomorrow is my day off." (The next day was Friday. Mommy was going to be at home.) "We will bake a whole pie on Monday."

"Can we use the crust we just made?" I asked.

"Yes, we can," said Merry.

I was worried about the crust. Would it still be good on Monday? Luckily Merry knew what to do. She told us to shape the crust into a big ball. Then she wrapped it in aluminum foil and put it in the freezer.

"The dough will keep that way," Merry assured me. "We can use it on Monday to make the crust."

Merry left as soon as Mommy came home. It was when I was helping Mommy set the table for dinner that I had an idea. A brilliant idea. I would write my essay about Merry. That way no one in my family would feel left out if I did not write about them. And besides, I was thankful to Merry for so many things. If not for her, I would not know how to bake a pie, make a vase, or play the kazoo.

I told Mommy about the essay contest and how I was going to write about Merry. Mommy liked my idea a lot.

"What are you going to do to show Merry how grateful you are to her?" Mommy asked.

"Oh, that part is easy," I answered. "I will make Merry a pie for her Thanksgiving dinner all by myself. After she teaches me, of course." Mommy laughed. "Please do not tell Merry I am writing about her," I went on. "I want to surprise her with the pie."

"I will not say anything, Karen. I promise."

I was so excited about my idea that as soon as I finished setting the table, I went upstairs and began writing.

Grandparents, Uncles, and Aunts

Here is the essay I wrote and read to my class:

I AM THANKFUL FOR MERRY PERKINS, MY NANNY. MERRY CAME TO OUR HOUSE WHEN MOMMY DECIDED TO GO BACK TO WORK. MERRY TAKES CARE OF MY LITTLE BROTHER, ANDREW, AND ME EVERY AFTERNOON AFTER SCHOOL. I KNEW I WAS GOING TO LIKE MERRY RIGHT AWAY BECAUSE HER NAME SOUNDS LIKE MARY POPPINS. AND YOU KNOW, MERRY IS A LOT LIKE MARY POPPINS. SHE

TELLS US WONDERFUL STORIES, AND SHE MAKES ANIMALS APPEAR OUT OF CLAY. RIGHT NOW MERRY IS TEACHING US HOW TO BAKE A PUMPKIN PIE. MERRY IS MORE THAN A TEACHER AND A NANNY. SHE IS ALSO MY FRIEND. I CAN TALK TO HER WHEN I AM UPSET, WHEN I AM HAPPY, OR WHEN I AM IN A BAD MOOD, AND SHE ALWAYS UNDERSTANDS.

TO SHOW MERRY HOW GRATEFUL I AM TO HER, I AM GOING TO MAKE HER A PUMPKIN PIE. MERRY IS SUCH A GOOD TEACHER THAT I AM SURE MY PIE WILL TURN OUT WELL. I WILL GIVE HER THE PIE RIGHT BEFORE THANKSGIVING.

When I was finished reading, everyone clapped. Even Ms. Colman. In fact, my class clapped after almost every presentation. We laughed and laughed when Ricky told us about his aunt Mabel and Bumper, his cocker spaniel. Ricky made Bumper sound like the hardest dog in the world to train. Ricky's parents did not even want to keep Bumper because he kept jumping up on the dining room table to knock the food to the floor. Ricky's aunt had to keep Bumper

29

at her house while he went to obedience school.

Tammy talked about her uncle who is an actor and a director. He once let Tammy act in *The Wizard of Oz*. She played one of the Munchkins.

Almost all the kids talked about someone in their family. Except Nancy and me. Nancy wrote about her ballet teacher, Mrs. Flament. Nancy said she would make up a dance and perform it, to show her thanks.

The last person to read her essay was Pamela Harding. She bragged about her grandparents who live in Florida and sail their boat a lot. Pamela is going to go visit them this spring, by herself. And her grandmother has promised she will teach Pamela how to sail. Pamela said she would do the dinner dishes every night while she was visiting. That was how she would show how grateful she was. Even though I do not like Pamela much, I did like her essay.

When Pamela sat down, Ms. Colman clapped for all the presentations. She told us they were the best essays she had ever heard from a group of second-graders. When my class heard that, we clapped too. We were still making a lot of noise when Ms. Colman collected our essays so she could send them in for the contest. We did not calm down until Ms. Colman told us she had an announcement to make.

Another announcement?

"This year there will be a special school assembly on the Monday before Thanksgiving," Ms. Colman began. "Every class is expected to perform something in it."

Everyone had a lot of ideas about what we could do. I suggested putting on a Thanksgiving play. Nancy wanted us to dance. Omar said we should tell Pilgrim jokes. Bobby and Ian thought we could dress as superheroes and run around onstage, pretending to save people.

Ms. Colman said those were good ideas, but that over the weekend we should think some more about what we wanted to do. This was going to be fun.

Gourds, Corn, and Squash

I spent most of Saturday and Sunday thinking about the assembly. By Sunday afternoon I still did not have any great ideas. Neither did Nancy. She was at my house. We were sitting on my bed, thinking. Goosie was in my lap. He was no help either.

"We could sing a Thanksgiving song," I suggested.

"We could," said Nancy. She did not sound very excited.

"We could dress up as Pilgrims," I began.

"Everybody will probably be doing something like that," Nancy said.

"I know, but wait, remember when Ms. Colman said we made wonderful presentations?"

"Yeah."

"Well, we could read our essays aloud at the assembly," I finished.

"Dressed in Pilgrim costumes?" asked Nancy.

"Yes," I said, trying to sound more excited than I felt.

"I do not know, Karen," Nancy said. "It took us a long time to read all those essays in class. The kids at the assembly might get bored if we read all of them."

Nancy had a point. But at least I had something to suggest in class the next day.

"Girls!"

Mommy was calling us from downstairs. She wanted to know if we would help her decorate the house for Thanksgiving.

"Sure," Nancy said.

I was happy to go downstairs too. For once I was tired of thinking.

Mommy had bought dried corn, gourds, and squash at the farmers' market. Nancy and I hung some dried corn on the front door. We used three cobs of corn and hung them with their tops bunched together. I wanted to put even more corn on the door. But Nancy and Mommy said it looked good the way it was.

Nancy and I also helped Mommy make a decoration for the dining room table. (Mommy called it a centerpiece.) To make it, we picked out one of Mommy's prettiest bowls. Then we put squashes and gourds inside it. I chose a lot of the greenish gourds with white speckles. Nancy liked the yellow ones.

When we were done, I thought our centerpiece looked gigundoly beautiful.

"Almost good enough to eat," Nancy re-marked.

"If you like squash," I said, wrinkling my nose. Nancy laughed.

Decorating was fun. But I was glad that this year, I would have a more important job for Thanksgiving — baking the pie.

And the Winner Is . . .

On Monday I was all set to tell my class my idea for the assembly. But just as I began talking, someone knocked on the door of our classroom.

"Now who could that be?" Ms. Colman wondered.

The door opened. Mrs. Titus, our principal, poked her head inside and asked if Ms. Colman could come talk to her right away.

I was a little worried. I hoped nothing was wrong.

Ms. Colman was only gone for a minute.

When she came back to our classroom she was smiling.

"Class, I have some wonderful news," Ms. Colman announced. "As you know, I sent your essays to the historical society last Friday."

I nodded a little impatiently. I wished Ms. Colman would hurry up and tell us what the wonderful news was.

"Well, the society liked your essays so much, they have awarded you — the whole class — the grand prize."

"The grand prize?" Ricky repeated. Some of the kids in the back of the room began cheering.

I stared at my teacher with my mouth open. "You mean we all won?" I asked. I had to talk loudly so Ms. Colman could hear me. For once, she did not tell me to use my indoor voice.

"Yes, the whole class won," Ms. Colman said, beaming. "The historical society had intended to give the grand prize to just one person, but then they opened the envelope with all your essays in it and the society thought they were the best."

"Wow," Hannie exclaimed.

"What is the grand prize?" Bobby asked.

"I do not know," Ms. Colman answered. "But we are going to find out tomorrow when we visit the historical society."

Some of the kids groaned a little when they heard that we would have to wait. But I was so excited that we had won that I did not mind *too* much. It took my class a long time to settle down after that exciting news.

At recess all we could talk about was the prize. "We probably won something to do with Thanksgiving," Ricky guessed.

"Why do you think that?" asked Hank. He was holding a kickball. But no one wanted to play.

"Because we had to write about Thanksgiving, remember?" Pamela said in a meanie-mo voice. Her arms were folded across her chest.

"Maybe we won a trip to Plymouth Rock

in Massachusetts," I blurted out. "That is where the Pilgrims landed when they came here from England."

"We know that, Karen," said Leslie.

"I do not think so," said Tammy. "I bet we won tickets to a play or a concert."

"I hope not," I said.

Tammy gave me a funny look.

"I like plays and concerts a lot," I explained. "But if we won tickets, how would we ever decide who got to go?"

"Maybe we won twenty tickets?" Terri suggested hopefully.

"I do not think so," said Sara, just as the bell rang. That meant recess was over. Boo and bullfrogs.

After school that day, I rushed right into the kitchen. I could not wait to tell Merry and Andrew my exciting news. Then I remembered something important. I could not tell Merry about the essay contest yet. I wanted it to be a surprise.

"Karen, we are making piecrust again,"

Andrew said. "Merry wants to teach us how to do it better."

"Okay," I said. "But I think I will do my homework upstairs."

Merry gave me a funny look. "After my snack," I added.

I would have liked to cook. But I was afraid I would give away the surprise. Besides, Andrew needed a lot more help with cooking than I did.

The Grand Prize

The next morning, I could not wait to go to school. I wondered when we would go to the historical society. Ms. Colman had said that a bus would take us. It would be the same bus that takes us on our field trips.

Luckily, my class did not have to wait long. I took attendance (yea!). And right after I finished, Ms. Colman told us to put on our coats and line up outside. The bus was already here.

"I love the words *grand prize*," said Audrey. She sat next to me on the bus.

"They do sound good," I agreed.

"I just wonder what our prize will be," said Hannie. She sat with Nancy across the aisle.

By the time we reached downtown Stoneybrook, my class had guessed everything from a Pilgrim costume to a set of books about the first Thanksgiving.

The bus pulled up to the curb in front of the brick building that belongs to the historical society. We were met by a woman dressed in a plaid suit. She said her name was Jane Kellogg.

"Ms. Kellogg is the president of the Stoneybrook Historical Society," Ms. Colman told us.

Inside, Ms. Kellogg led us down a hallway and into a room that looked like it could be someone's living room. Someone's *fancy* living room. A big chandelier, made of glass, hung from the ceiling. A huge Oriental rug covered the floor. And all around were antique chairs on spindly legs and little tables with marble tops. The furniture looked almost too good to sit on.

"This place looks like a museum," I whispered to Hannie.

"It is a museum," Hannie whispered back.

In the big room, more people congratulated us. A tall woman wearing lots of jewelry shook Ms. Colman's hand. "I am Mrs. Vanderbellen," the woman said. "I host charity dinners for the society. It is so marvelous the children truly understand the meaning of Thanksgiving."

"Indeed," said a gray-haired man, smiling at us.

"That's Mr. Powers," Hannie told me. "My dad knows him. He writes for the *Stoneybrook News*." (The *Stoneybrook News* is our local newspaper.)

"He does?" I said. "Do you think he is going to write a story about us?"

Just as I said that, a woman with red hair snapped our picture. I smiled at the camera while she took a few more shots.

Then Ms. Kellogg announced we were going outside again. "I am sure you are eager to see your prize," she added.

"Our prize is outside?" Ricky sounded surprised.

"Yes, it is," answered Ms. Kellogg as we followed her out the door. She led us around to the back of the building.

"What do you think is waiting for us in the backyard?" Hannie asked me.

For once I did not know what to say. But I could not wait to find out. Neither could the other kids. By the time we reached the back of the building, it seemed as if my class were holding its breath.

We followed Ms. Kellogg toward a small pen covered with chicken wire. Whatever was inside the pen started making strange loud noises.

"Here is your prize," I heard Ms. Kellogg say. I could not see the prize right away because I was at the back of the line. But I heard Pamela Harding say, "A turkey? We won a turkey?"

A *live* turkey? I was shocked. For a few

seconds no one said anything, not even Ms. Colman. Instead we gathered around the turkey's pen and just looked at it. Our turkey had a long wrinkly neck — a neck that was beginning to turn red.

"That means it is getting excited," said Addie. (Addie knows a lot about animals, because her mother is an animal doctor.)

The turkey ruffled its feathers and hopped around in its cage. It even began flapping its wings.

"It probably is not used to all this attention," Ms. Colman remarked.

"Is it a boy turkey or a girl turkey?" I wanted to know.

"It's a boy," Jane Kellogg answered.

"I cannot believe we won a turkey," said Omar.

Jane Kellogg agreed that a turkey was probably not the best prize for our class, but she hoped we would enjoy it anyway. "We thought only one person would win the grand prize," she added.

"What are we going to do with a turkey?" Hannie wondered aloud.

"He could be our class pet," Ian suggested. Just as Ian said that, the turkey began gobbling.

"He would be a pretty noisy pet," said Audrey. "Besides, we already have Hootie."

"Turkeys should be kept outside anyway," Addie said.

"We could always cook him for Thanksgiving dinner," Pamela suggested.

"Very funny," said Ricky.

"The turkey will be delivered to your school this afternoon," Ms. Kellogg said.

"That gives us time to find a name and maybe decide what we are going to do with him," Ms. Colman replied. She still looked a little shocked.

We could hear our turkey gobbling in its pen when we left.

The Prize Arrives

"I think we should call the turkey Marmaduke," I said.

"What about Gobble Gobble?" asked Bobby.

"Or Big Tom?" suggested Ian.

"I think Tom is a boring name," Jannie remarked.

We were in our classroom, trying to think of a name for our turkey. Ms. Colman was writing down our suggestions on the board. This is what she had written so far:

Archie
Rojo (that means red in Spanish)
Harry
Larry
Marmaduke
Gobble Gobble
Big Tom

"If no one else has any suggestions, I think we should vote," Ms. Colman said. No one had any more ideas. So Ms. Colman asked for a show of hands after each name. And guess what? Only two people voted for Marmaduke. Ricky and me.

The name my class liked best was . . . Archie. I was disappointed. But I guessed I could get used to Archie — in time. At least Hannie would be happy. She was the one who suggested Archie.

"When is our turkey coming?" Ian wanted to know.

"Sometime this afternoon," Ms. Colman answered. "All too soon, because I still do not know what we are going to do with him."

I was getting an idea. Another of my brilliant ideas. I waved my hand in the air.

"Archie could star in our part of the assembly!" I suggested when Ms. Colman called on me.

"Yes!" said Bobby.

"With a real, live turkey, our piece will be the best in the school," I added.

"And the noisiest," said Pamela. She did not sound thrilled with my idea. But I did not care. I knew it was better than the Pilgrim idea I had had before.

"That is a wonderful suggestion, Karen," said Ms. Colman. "But we still have a problem."

"We do?" I asked.

Ms. Colman nodded. "The assembly is next Monday, almost a week away. We have nowhere to keep Archie in the meantime. I do not think he will be allowed to stay at school for more than a couple of days."

"Why not?" Hank wanted to know.

"He is too noisy, and he will disturb the other students and teachers," Ms. Colman answered gently. "Our most important job will be finding a place for Archie to live."

"But can he still be in the assembly?" I wanted to know.

"Yes, if we can find someone to take him for a little while, just until we can find a permanent home for him."

"I could ask my mother," said Addie. "But I do not think she will let me."

"I will ask Mommy and Seth," I said. "They let me bring Hootie home for a week."

Just then Mr. Fitzwater knocked on our door. (Mr. Fitzwater is our school custodian.) "A live turkey just arrived for this class," he announced. He stood in the doorway scratching his head. "The turkey is making quite a racket," he added. "Mrs. Titus does not want me to bring him inside."

"I am not surprised," said Ms. Colman. "We will come outside to help you."

"Thanks," said Mr. Fitzwater. He looked relieved.

We found Archie sitting in a cage in the school courtyard. When he saw us, Archie ruffled his feathers and gobbled. Several teachers looked out their windows. The fifth-graders who were coming in from recess stopped to stare at Archie. So did their teacher, Ms. Kushel.

"What is a turkey doing here?" asked one girl.

"His name is Archie," I said. "My class won him in an essay contest."

"He was the grand prize," Ricky added.

"Really?" The girl looked kind of sorry for us. "What was the second prize?"

"Two turkeys," Mr. Counts joked. (Mr. Counts is the school librarian. He had come outside to see what all the noise was about.)

By now Archie was gobbling louder than ever. His neck had turned bright red. And he kept banging his wings against the sides of the cage.

"We should do something," said Addie. "He is going to hurt himself."

Mr. Fitzwater and Mr. Counts told Ms. Colman they would set up a pen in the school yard to keep Archie safe for now. "We need to get him out of that little cage," Mr. Counts said.

"I agree," said Ms. Colman.

Then Mrs. Titus came outside. First she congratulated us on our prizewinning essays. "I am so proud of you," she said. But then she gave us some bad news. She told us our turkey could not stay at school. "We can keep him only for a few days at most," she announced. "He is too noisy. This is a school, not a zoo."

"I understand," said Ms. Colman.

Archie Needs a Home

"I know a turkey is not like a guinea pig," I told Nancy as we walked home from the bus stop that afternoon. "Archie will be a lot harder to take care of than Hootie was."

Nancy agreed. "And you will probably have to keep him outside. He might scare Rocky and Midgie."

"But Archie is not really a pet," I said. "He is a turkey. I hope Mommy and Seth will let me keep him."

"I hope so too. You can always tell them your next-door neighbors will not mind if he makes noise outside," Nancy said as we waved good-bye.

I laughed.

"Merry, Andrew, guess what?" I said as soon as I came in my house.

"What?" Andrew wanted to know. He sat at the kitchen table eating pretzels and apple slices.

I sat down with him and told Merry and Andrew all about Archie. I explained that my class had won him in an essay contest. But I remembered not to tell Merry what my essay was about. I still wanted to surprise her. "We would need to keep Archie only for a few days," I finished. "Just until the assembly."

"A real turkey, here." Andrew sounded pleased.

"Karen, you never told me your class won the grand prize in an essay contest." Merry sounded very impressed.

I nodded. "Yeah," I said, shrugging.

"A turkey is a strange prize," said Merry.

"But if you want to keep him here for awhile, I will try to help you."

"Oh, thanks, Merry," I said, beaming.

"The first thing we should do is go to the library to check out some books on turkeys," Merry suggested.

I wished I had thought of that.

At the library, I found a book called *All About Turkeys*. I also read about turkeys in the encyclopedia. By the time we left, I had become an expert on turkeys.

Mommy and Seth were just pulling into the driveway when Merry, Andrew, and I returned home. I waited for them to come in the house and take off their coats. Then Mommy talked to Merry, and Seth played with Andrew. Everyone seemed to be in a good mood. Now was the perfect time to ask about Archie.

But guess what?

Mommy and Seth said no. At the same time. Then Mommy repeated her no. "Karen, we already have a cat, a dog, and a

part-time rat and hermit crab. This house is too small for another animal, especially a turkey," Mommy added.

"But the turkey would live outside, in a pen in the backyard," I pleaded. "And only until our assembly."

"If he is too noisy for your school yard, he is probably too noisy for the backyard," Mommy said. "He will disturb the neighbors."

"He will not bother Nancy's family. Nancy said so. And they are right next door."

"No," Mommy repeated.

"I will take care of Archie all by myself," I insisted. "You will not have to do anything. I have been reading about turkeys." I waved my library book under her nose. "Archie just needs to eat seeds and nuts or leftover corn."

"I will help take care of Archie too," Andrew promised.

"And I will do all I can," said Merry, just before she left.

"Let me think about it," said Mommy.

At dinner Mommy asked me about Archie again. I told her he was not as big as most male turkeys, and that he got excited when there were a lot of people around. "It would be better for him to be someplace quiet like our backyard," I said.

"And it would be for only a few days, right?" Mommy wanted to know.

I nodded. "Ms. Colman said she would try to find Archie a home to go to after our assembly. Archie is going to be the star of our assembly," I pointed out again. "If he is not there, our part of the show will be ruined." I wrung my hands.

Mommy and Seth were impressed at how much I knew about turkeys. I knew where turkeys live, where they sleep, and how fast they can run.

"Can Archie fly?" Mommy wanted to know.

"No," I answered. "Wild turkeys can fly, but Archie is not a wild turkey."

Finally, when we were eating dessert,

Mommy said yes, we could keep Archie. "Just for a few days, Karen."

Seth said he would clear a space for Archie's pen in the backyard.

"Thank you," I cried, hugging them both. "My class will be so happy. So will Ms. Colman. And so will Archie."

After dinner Mommy called Ms. Colman. I heard her say Merry would pick up Archie on Thursday. That meant he would have to spend only one more night at school. Just enough time to plan our part in the assembly. I wondered if Archie were ready for a rehearsal.

Turkey in the Straw

The next morning, I visited Archie before school started. He gobbled a little when he saw me coming. But he seemed calmer than the day before. He bobbed his head at me. It almost looked as if he were saying hello.

My class cheered when Ms. Colman told them I could take Archie home.

"I am allowed to keep him only until the assembly," I said.

"Still, that is better than nothing," Addie remarked.

"We need to spend some time this morning finding a home for Archie," Ms. Colman announced. She began writing the names and addresses of nearby zoos and farms on the board. "I would like you to pick one of the places on the board and write a letter asking if they could take in a turkey," Ms. Colman said. Then she passed around fancy white paper and envelopes. (The paper had no lines on it.)

Ms. Colman made sure we each wrote to a different place. I decided to write my letter to one of the zoos. I had no idea there were so many farms and zoos near Stoneybrook. "Some of these places are wildlife preserves," Ms. Colman explained. "They shelter animals so no one can harm them."

I wrote my letter in my notebook first so I would not have to cross out anything on the fancy paper. When I was finished, I showed my letter to Ms. Colman and Ricky. They liked it a lot.

This is what I wrote:

DEAR STONEYBROOK WILDLIFE PRESERVE:
   OUR SECOND-GRADE CLASS WON A TURKEY
WHOSE NAME IS ARCHIE. WE LIKE ARCHIE VERY
MUCH. BUT WE CANNOT KEEP HIM AT OUR
SCHOOL. AND NO ONE IN MY CLASS IS ALLOWED TO
BRING ARCHIE HOME FOR MORE THAN A FEW
DAYS. ARCHIE NEEDS A REAL HOME WITH OTHER
TURKEYS TO KEEP HIM COMPANY. HE IS USED TO
LIVING OUTSIDE.
   I HOPE YOU WILL TAKE ARCHIE. AND IF YOU
DO, I HOPE YOU LET ME COME TO SEE HIM. I
WOULD LIKE TO VISIT ARCHIE ON SPECIAL HOLI-
DAYS LIKE THANKSGIVING AND CHRISTMAS.
   SINCERELY,
   KAREN BREWER
   STONEYBROOK ACADEMY

My class spent a long time on our letters.
When we were finished, Ms. Colman collected them to take to the post office.

"Before we begin our geography lesson,

class, I think we should talk about the assembly."

I was very glad Ms. Colman said that. I had been thinking about the assembly quite a bit. "Archie should be the star of our act," I said.

"I agree," said Ms. Colman. "But what would you like to do with Archie?"

"We could pretend to catch him for our Thanksgiving dinner," Pamela suggested.

"Yeah, and just as we sit down to eat, the turkey walks away," said Hannie.

"I like that idea," said Bobby.

Ms. Colman did not.

Finally, after a lot of talking, we decided to let Archie strut around onstage while we sang "Turkey in the Straw" and danced. Luckily almost everyone in my class knew the song. But Omar, Bobby, and Hank were not happy about dancing. Especially when Nancy suggested teaching them fancy twirls.

Ms. Colman said we might not have time

to learn anything too complicated before the assembly.

"Maybe we should just dance around on-stage to the music," Audrey suggested.

Everyone but Nancy liked that idea. I did not think our dance mattered too much. Archie would steal the show, no matter what we did.

Smile for the Camera

After our math lesson the next morning, Ms. Colman said, "Class, I have some exciting news."

"More exciting news," Ricky whispered.

"Oh, goody!" whispered Natalie.

"Shhh," I said. I did not want to miss a word.

"The *Stoneybrook News* will be publishing an article about your essays in a special Thanksgiving edition," Ms. Colman continued. "The paper will be printing all your essays."

My class clapped and cheered almost as loudly as when we heard we had won the contest.

I was excited about seeing my name in print in a real newspaper. But I was also a little disappointed. Now my big surprise for Merry would be no surprise at all. I decided I would have to tell Merry about my essay before that special edition came out. That way she would hear the news from me first.

Ms. Colman let us practice for the assembly after recess. She wrote the words to "Turkey in the Straw" on the blackboard. Then she hummed the tune. We sang the song twice. It sounded strange without music. Ms. Colman said our next rehearsal would take place in the auditorium with our music teacher playing the piano.

That afternoon Merry came to school with Andrew to pick up Archie and me in her car. Mr. Fitzwater had already put Archie back in his cage and had taken down his pen so we could put it up in our backyard.

Merry told Mr. Fitzwater that we did not need the pen. Seth is a carpenter, and he had already built a new pen for Archie. We just needed to put chicken wire around it when we got home.

Everyone in my class came outside with Ms. Colman to say good-bye to Archie.

"You will see him soon," I said as Mr. Fitzwater carried Archie's cage to our car. "The assembly is in four days."

Andrew and I squeezed in beside Archie's cage on the backseat. On the way home, Archie seemed nervous. His throat and head turned bright red.

At home, I helped Merry carry Archie's cage to the backyard. He was heavy! We left Archie in his cage while Merry put the chicken wire around Archie's pen. Archie seemed calmer now. He was not fluffing up his wings or gobbling crossly. Andrew and I gave him food and water. Then, when his pen was ready, we let him out of his cage so he could walk around our yard. Merry tried to take his picture, with Andrew and me posing on either side of him. Archie did not like the camera. But I think we got some gigundoly funny pictures.

Soon it started to grow dark. We put Archie in his pen and fastened the gate just as Seth's car pulled into the driveway.

"Time to go inside and wash up," Merry told us. It was almost dinnertime. We had missed another chance to bake pies with Merry. Boo and bullfrogs! But I knew we still had time before Thanksgiving. Besides, what could be more fun than spending the afternoon playing with a turkey?

After Merry left, I remembered that I had not told her about my surprise yet. I wanted to be sure to tell her the next day.

The Runaway

The next morning at school, Ms. Colman had bad news for us. "No one will take Archie," she announced. "I called more farms and zoos yesterday after school. The farms have too many turkeys already, and the zoos do not want them."

"Why not?" asked Addie.

"People do not go to zoos to see turkeys," answered Ms. Colman. "They go to see more unusual animals."

"Has anyone answered our letters yet?" asked Pamela.

Ms. Colman shook her head. "No. Not yet."

I sighed. I knew Mommy and Seth would not let me keep Archie forever. And I would hate to see him move to a place that did not really want him. A place where he would be unhappy. I was so worried about Archie that I had trouble paying attention during our rehearsal that morning. We were practicing onstage in the auditorium with Mrs. Noonan, our music teacher. Ms. Colman watched.

We sang the song about five times while Mrs. Noonan played the piano. Then we practiced dancing onstage to the music. That was fun.

"Now we will practice singing and dancing at the same time," said Mrs. Noonan.

"We are not really dancing," Nancy whispered to me. "We are just stomping around." (Nancy is very serious about dancing.)

I shrugged. "When Archie comes onstage, we may not be able to do any more than that. We will be very busy trying not to step on him."

"Class, are you ready?" called Mrs. Noonan.

"Yes," some of us answered.

Mrs. Noonan began playing. We started singing. And dancing. I bumped into Ricky. Omar and Hank crashed into each other. Pamela stepped on Audrey's toes.

"Stop," said Mrs. Noonan. She walked onto the stage and moved us around so we were not standing so close together. She also separated Hank, Bobby, and Omar. We tried again. And again. And again. By the sixth try, Mrs. Noonan was satisfied. Sort of. She said we should try to practice in class once more before the assembly.

I rushed home from the bus stop that afternoon. "Archie, did you miss me?" I called as I ran into my backyard. Archie did not make a sound.

"Archie?" I called again. I stopped in front of his pen. Archie was not inside. "Archie?" I looked around the pen, then around the yard. There was no sign of my turkey — anywhere.

"What happened to Archie?" I cried as I opened the front door.

Merry sat at the kitchen table with Andrew. Andrew looked as though he had been crying.

"Archie is gone," Merry told me. "I am very sorry, Karen. I think I might have left the door to his pen open by mistake when we fed him at lunchtime."

"What?" I shrieked.

"We noticed he was gone about fifteen minutes ago," Merry said.

"Fifteen minutes ago! And you are just sitting here not looking for him?" I was furious with Merry. How could she have been so careless?

"I called your mother at work," said Merry. "She is going to come home to help us look. I am very, very sorry about this, Karen."

I glared at Merry. I was too mad to talk to her anymore. Instead I stomped upstairs to wait for Mommy.

"Merry has ruined Thanksgiving. And our assembly," I told Mommy when she came home. (I still was not talking to Merry.)

"Karen, it was an accident," said Mommy. "Merry did not do this on purpose. She feels just as bad about what happened as you do."

"No one feels as bad as I do," I said. "Archie could be in danger. If anything happens to him, it will be all Merry's fault."

"Now, Karen," said Mommy, "I know you feel awful. But it is unfair to blame Merry."

No matter what Mommy said, I could not forgive Merry. I was sorry I ever wrote my essay about her.

Merry stayed with Andrew while Mommy and I walked around the neighborhood looking for Archie. We walked for a long time. We asked everyone we met about Archie. No one had seen him.

When it started growing dark, Mommy said we had to go home. "Archie will be too hard to find now."

I burst into tears. "We will continue our search tomorrow," Mommy promised.

"First thing tomorrow," I said.

Missing: One Live Turkey

I tossed and turned all night. How could I sleep, knowing Archie was missing? Would he find food? Would he stay away from foxes and stray dogs? The more I thought about Archie all alone outside in the dark, the more worried I became.

I must have fallen asleep, because when I opened my eyes, the sun was shining into my room. I sprang out of bed and ran downstairs.

"Mommy, Seth, what time is it?"

"About seven o'clock," answered Mommy.

"You let me sleep this late when Archie is missing? How could you?"

"We were planning our search," said Seth. He showed me the MISSING TURKEY fliers he had made. He had drawn a picture of Archie and written MISSING TURKEY in big letters at the top. On the bottom was more information about Archie and our phone number.

"These fliers look nice," I said.

"We should post these around town," Seth said.

"And we should carry food, plus something to put Archie in if we find him," Mommy added.

"What do you mean *if* we find him?" I said. "We have to find him. I am going to call Hannie and Nancy. They will help us."

"Good idea," said Seth.

I called Hannie and Nancy while Mommy, Seth, and Andrew ate breakfast. They said they would be right over. I also called the big house and talked to Kristy. She told me she would come help too.

Nancy arrived first with her mother. Then Hannie arrived with her father. A few minutes later, Kristy arrived with Sam, Charlie, and David Michael. Kristy had brought over a cardboard box with holes punched in it, for carrying Archie, and a packet of seeds for him to eat. (Kristy is very organized.)

Mommy and Seth divided us into groups. I was with Mommy, Hannie, and Nancy. The plan was for each group to walk to a different part of town to look for Archie. Each group took food Archie would like and something to carry Archie in. I took Archie's seeds and box in my red wagon.

"Turkeys can run fast," I said. "Archie might be pretty far away by now."

"I doubt he went too far," said Seth.

I hoped Seth was right. While the grownups planned where we should go, Hannie, Nancy, Kristy, and I put up some fliers in our neighborhood.

When we came home, everyone was ready to go. Mommy, Hannie, Nancy, and I began by knocking on our neighbors' doors.

"We are looking for a missing turkey," Mommy explained to Mr. Drucker. He was the first one who answered our knock. "We were wondering if he might be in your backyard. We do not think he went very far."

Everyone we talked to was happy to let us look around their yards. We walked through big yards and little yards. Yards with swing sets, slides, and sandboxes. Yards with trees and shrubs. Yards with pools. Yards with flower beds and vegetable gardens. There was no sign of Archie anywhere.

The Search Goes On

Mommy, Hannie, Nancy, and I spent almost the whole morning searching on our street.

When we started down Main Street, I saw Ricky and Mr. Torres walking toward us. "Oh, no." I moaned. "Should we tell them Archie is missing?"

"Yes, I think so," said Hannie. "They can help us look."

"I guess they could," I said, sighing. "But I am sooo embarrassed. I hope they will not blame me."

"Why should they? It is not your fault," said Nancy.

"I know," I said. "This is Merry's fault."

You know what? Ricky did not seem mad at all. In fact, he already knew Archie was missing, because he had seen our fliers. He and his dad said they would start looking on Spring Street.

Mommy, Hannie, Nancy, and I went to the Stoneybrook Community Center to look in their yard, which is huge. At the community center we ran into more kids from my class. Omar and Hank were playing basketball with Omar's father. They stopped their game to help us look. So did Audrey, Terri, and Tammy, who were out on their in-line skates.

"I am sooo mad at Merry," I told Audrey. "I wish I had never written my essay about her. I do not know what I will do if she calls to thank me after she reads it in the paper." Audrey just looked at me. "Unless we find Archie, our assembly will be ruined," I added.

"I bet we will find him," said Audrey as she unbuckled her skates.

I handed Audrey some fliers. She said she would go with Tammy and Terri and their mother to look for Archie on Rosedale Road.

By now it was lunchtime, but I did not want to stop looking.

"We could always eat some of Archie's food," joked Hannie.

"Very funny," I said.

"How about getting some pizza slices to go from Pizza Express," Mommy suggested.

I usually love the pizza at Pizza Express. But today I was not in the mood. I also could not wait to get away from downtown Stoneybrook. It was embarrassing to run into so many kids from my class and have to tell them Archie was missing. I just hoped we would not see Pamela. I could only imagine what she would say.

We did not have to wait long for our pizza slices. I looked around Pizza Express. No sign of Pamela. Or Leslie and Jannie. "I guess we could eat here," I said. "Maybe at the counter."

"Maybe we could eat while we walk," said Hannie. "We will not waste any time that way."

"Okay," I said.

I was very happy when Mommy suggested we look beyond Stoneybrook. "Your friends are taking care of the streets we were supposed to cover," Mommy added.

On our way home to get Mommy's car, we did meet someone. Not Pamela, thank goodness. But a reporter from the *Stoneybrook News*. He had seen our fliers and talked to some of the kids in the other search parties. He wanted to write a story about the runaway turkey.

Uh-oh. Now everyone in Stoneybrook would know that my family lost Archie.

"The publicity will be good," said Mommy. "Maybe someone who reads about Archie will give him a home. We are looking for a permanent home for the turkey," Mommy told the reporter.

"If we ever find him," I said glumly.

"This article should help you," said the reporter. "People who see Archie will read this story and call the newspaper."

I had not thought of that.

After we said good-bye to the reporter, we went home and put our box and our seeds in Mommy's car. Then we drove until we reached the part of Stoneybrook that looks like the country.

"Why don't we look for Archie on some farms?" Mommy suggested.

"Okay," I said, even though I did not think we would find Archie anywhere.

"Would Archie go this far?" Nancy wanted to know.

"Turkeys can run fast," I said. "Some can go about twenty miles an hour."

"Really?" said Hannie.

Nancy looked very impressed.

"So," I said sadly, "Archie could be anywhere. This is hopeless."

"Oh, Karen, we will find him," said Hannie. But she did not look too sure anymore.

Mommy made a left turn and drove up a long dirt road.

"This is the Stones' farm," I said as Mommy stopped the car by a shiny tractor, near the barn.

"It is," said Mommy.

I like the Stones' farm a lot. Hannie, Nancy, and I went to Farm Camp there once.

We saw chickens in the yard, but no turkey. I walked around the chicken coop. And that is when I saw a turkey. A real, live turkey eating berries under a tree! It was the first turkey I had seen all day.

"Archie!" I cried as I ran toward him.

The turkey lifted his head and started running. I chased after him yelling, "Archie, Archie, come back!" But the turkey only ran faster.

"I do not know if it really was Archie," I told Hannie and Nancy when they caught up to me. "But it could have been." Just seeing a turkey had made me feel better.

"The Stones' pickup truck is gone,"

Mommy reported. "They must not be home."

"So we cannot ask them about Archie," I said.

"Not now," Mommy answered.

I did not want to go home, but Mommy said it was time to leave. When we returned home Seth, Kristy, Sam, Charlie, David Michael, and Andrew were waiting for us. No one had seen Archie. No one had talked to anyone who had even seen him.

I sat down at the kitchen table and cried.

Merry's Surprise

I was not hungry the next morning either. Especially not when I noticed the newspaper, open to the page about my class. I did not feel thankful that my class had won a turkey. And I was not at all thankful for Merry. I did not even want to see the article.

The phone rang. I heard Mommy answer it in the study.

"Karen, it is for you," Mommy called after a few minutes.

"Hello," I said when I picked up the phone.

"Hello, Karen." Merry's voice was loud and clear.

I frowned and did not answer. Merry was the last person I wanted to talk to.

"Karen?" said Merry.

"Yes," I said after a long pause.

"I have a surprise for you," said Merry.

"Oh," I said in a flat voice.

"Your mother is going to drive you over to my house to see it."

"She is?" I did not want to go to Merry's house.

"I hope you will come," Merry said.

"Uh, maybe. I will talk to Mommy about it." I figured Merry wanted to thank me for the essay I had written about her. The only problem was, I was not thankful for Merry anymore. And I did not want to see her. I was sure I would say something awful to her.

"See you soon, then," said Merry.

"Good-bye," I said.

"Finish your breakfast before we go, Karen," said Mommy.

"I am not hungry. And I do not want to go to Merry's house," I said with my hands on my hips.

"Karen, I think you are going to like Merry's surprise," said Mommy.

"I will not."

Mommy took a deep breath. "Karen, we are going to Merry's," she said firmly. Then she gave me a look. I sighed and sat down to finish my breakfast.

On the way to Merry's I worried about what I would say to her. I decided maybe it would be better not to talk at all. (Even though that is very hard for me.)

Merry lived in a small gray house with a red door. I had to admit that I was (a little) excited about seeing where she lived. I had never been to her house.

Mommy rang the doorbell. Merry opened her door and smiled at us. Her house smelled like pancakes and flowers. "Come in," she said, holding her door open wide.

Mommy and I followed Merry through a sunny living room filled with plants.

We stopped outside the kitchen. Merry's kitchen was closed off with a wooden gate.

"Do you have a pet?" I asked, looking at the gate. Then my mouth dropped opened.

There, in the middle of Merry's kitchen, was Archie.

A Welcome Phone Call

"Archie!" I shrieked.

Archie gobbled. I really think he was happy to see me. And I was so relieved, I could have hugged him.

"Where did you find him?" I asked Merry. (I forgot about not talking to her.)

"Archie found me," said Merry. "He was under one of my bird feeders this morning. I saw him when I brought in the newspaper. And speaking of the newspaper, Karen, I loved your essay. I was so touched that you wrote about me. Thank you."

"Oh, it was nothing," I said modestly. But I was pleased Merry had liked my essay so much. And when Merry held out her arms to hug me, I ran to her. And I forgave her. After all, she had found Archie. And she really is a great nanny.

"Was it hard to bring Archie indoors?" asked Mommy.

"I lured him inside with more birdseed," said Merry.

"He does not seem too upset about being in a house," I said.

"No, he is pretty calm," agreed Merry. "I was surprised."

"I hope he will not mind moving back to his pen in our backyard," I said. "Do we have anything to carry him in?"

"Yes, I brought his cage for the car trip home," said Mommy, smiling. "It's in the trunk."

"I am so glad you found Archie in time for our assembly tomorrow," I said.

"It was lucky he turned up," Merry agreed.

Before we left, Merry made Mommy and me blueberry pancakes to celebrate. And you know what? I was starving. We ate at a little round table in Merry's kitchen, next to Archie.

Archie complained when we put him in his cage to go home. "It will not be for long," I promised him. "I have to take you home. And tomorrow you will come to school with me."

Archie kept gobbling. But at least the drive home was short. And he seemed to like being back in his pen. I gave him water, dried corn, and berries. I made sure his gate was latched when I left. I did not want to take any more chances.

When I was in my house, I called Hannie, Nancy, and Kristy to tell them the good news. I even called Ms. Colman to tell her the assembly was saved. I was on the phone for a long time. I did not even notice there was a message for me by the phone until Andrew told me.

The message said, *Call Mrs. Stone.*

"Mrs. Stone?" I said out loud. I wondered why she wanted to talk to me.

I dialed Mrs. Stone's number. "Hello, Mrs. Stone?" I said when she picked up the phone. "This is Karen Brewer."

"Hello, Karen. I read about your missing turkey in the newspaper."

"Oh, we found Archie," I interrupted her.

"I am glad to hear that," said Mrs. Stone. And then Mrs. Stone told me the most wonderful news. She said she and Mr. Stone would like to give Archie a home on their farm. I could visit him whenever I wanted. Hooray!

I talked to Mrs. Stone for awhile. I told her all about Archie — what he likes to eat, what he sounds like, what he does when he is mad. Then Mommy talked to Mrs. Stone too. I heard her say that Merry and I would bring Archie to the Stones' farm after the assembly.

On Stage

"Did you find Archie yet?" asked Pamela.

It was Monday morning. I had just walked into my classroom. Archie was in a pen in the school courtyard. Mr. Fitzwater was outside with him. Mr. Fitzwater had said he would stay with Archie until I came out to take care of him.

"What happened to Archie?" asked Ian. "Did you lose him?"

"He ran away, but Karen found him!" shouted Hannie.

"My nanny, Merry, found him," I said. "Actually, he found her."

Just then Ms. Colman arrived. We rushed to our seats.

"Karen, maybe you should tell the class about Archie's adventure," Ms. Colman suggested.

I walked to the front of the classroom. "Merry, my nanny, left Archie's cage partway open Friday afternoon. She did that by mistake," I added. "Archie got out and ran away."

I talked for a long time. I told my class how we had looked all over Stoneybrook for Archie. And I named the people who had helped us. "Archie just turned up at Merry's bird feeder yesterday morning. Merry used birdseed to lead him into her kitchen. Then she put up a gate so he could not get away again."

"Where is Archie now?" Ricky wanted to know.

"Out in the yard," I answered, "in the pen Mr. Fitzwater set up for him."

"He is so quiet," Ricky remarked.

"The door to his pen is shut tight," I added. Everyone laughed.

"Oh, I have more news," I said.

"What?" asked Addie.

"Archie will have a new home — at Mrs. Stone's farm. We are taking him there after the assembly today."

"It was very nice of the Stones to offer Archie a home," Ms. Colman added. "They already have a lot of animals."

"But Archie is special," I said.

Ms. Colman announced that we had to rehearse our act again — with Archie. I went outside with Mr. Fitzwater to get Archie.

Soon it was time for the assembly. We changed into our costumes — jeans, flannel shirts, bandannas, and sneakers. Nancy, Hannie, and I stayed behind to wait with Archie. Everyone else went to the auditorium.

I fastened a rope around Archie's neck to lead him around. Then we waited. We could hear the other classes, but we could not see anything. One class sang "Over the River and Through the Wood."

"I wonder if they are doing a dance," said Nancy.

"If they are, I bet they do not have a live turkey dancing with them," I said.

It sounded like most of the classes were performing plays or reading stories aloud. Finally we heard Mr. Berger's class starting their play. That was our signal to lead Archie backstage.

Ms. Colman and the other kids were lined up, ready to go onstage.

"Get ready. Now!" said a sixth-grader, who was the stage manager.

My class walked out on the stage. I held Archie's rope. Then Mrs. Noonan began playing "Turkey in the Straw" on the piano.

My friends and I formed a circle around Archie and began singing and stomping to the music. I stomped to the front of the stage and Archie followed me. And then, the funniest thing happened: Archie started lifting up *his* feet and stomping around too!

102

I could hear the audience laughing and clapping. When we finished, the audience clapped and cheered some more. They even stood up. Nancy told me they were giving us a standing ovation.

I kept the rope around Archie's neck and led him outside after the show. Merry and Andrew were waiting for us.

As we drove away, I could see Ms. Colman and the kids from my class at the curb waving. "Good-bye, Archie," they called. Nancy and Hannie were trying very hard not to cry.

Mrs. Stone met us in front of her barn. "Thank you for giving Archie a home," I said as we set Archie's cage down.

"You are welcome, Karen. We will take good care of him, I promise," said Mrs. Stone.

When I said good-bye to Archie, I started to cry. I could not help it.

"You may visit whenever you want," said Mrs. Stone, patting me on the shoulder.

"I know," I said. I blew my nose with a pink tissue.

"I know you will miss him," said Merry. "But Archie will be happy here with the other animals."

I hoped he would be. I got in the car and turned in my seat. I waved and waved at Archie until he was out of sight.

Pumpkin Pie

When we arrived home, I looked at Archie's empty pen in the backyard. I missed seeing him there, eating the seeds I gave him.

Merry went into the kitchen to cut up apples for our snack. Suddenly I had an idea. "Do we still have the ingredients for a pumpkin pie?" I asked Merry.

"Yes, we do."

"I want to make a pie for you," I told Merry. "Just like I said I would in my essay."

"It's been so long since we made our

piecrust, Karen. Do you remember what I taught you?"

"Of course I do," I said.

So Merry sat in the kitchen and gave me directions. But I did everything myself. I measured out the ingredients for the filling and mixed them together. I rolled out the dough we had kept in the freezer. I fit the crust into the pie plate and crimped the edges. Then I poured in the filling. All Merry had to do was turn on the oven and put the pie in it. The pie smelled delicious when it was cooking. And when it was done, it looked perfect. (If I do say so myself.)

Andrew and I each had a little taste. We could not resist. But we gave the rest to Merry. She told us she would think of us when she ate it on Thanksgiving.

"We will think of you too," I said. "Especially when we are making our family's pie — by ourselves."

It was going to be a very happy and yummy Thanksgiving.

L. GODWIN

About the Author

ANN M. MARTIN lives in New York City and loves animals, especially cats. She has two cats of her own, Gussie and Woody.

Other books by Ann M. Martin that you might enjoy are *Stage Fright*; *Me and Katie (the Pest)*; and the books in *The Baby-sitters Club* series.

Ann likes ice cream and *I Love Lucy*. And she has her own little sister, whose name is Jane.

Little Sister

Don't miss #116

KAREN'S REINDEER

There was a line of trees at the back of the big-house yard. They looked beautiful in the moonlight with the snow on their branches. Then I frowned and squinted. I saw a big, dark shape moving through the trees. Was it a person? Somebody's dog?

No . . . it was too big to be a dog. It was even too big to be a person. Was it a bear?

Then the whatever-it-was stepped out from under the trees and into the moonlight. It was tall and a little shaggy, and it had antlers.

I could not believe my eyes. It was a reindeer. A real, live reindeer.

"Oh, my goodness!" I whispered to myself. A reindeer in my own backyard! Reindeer do not live in Connecticut. Reindeer live way up north, like at the . . . North Pole!